The Mystery of the Mountain Lion Tracks

A JUST JUNIPER Adventure

Sequel to JUST JUNIPER - The First Adventure

Go on more adventures with JUNIPER!

JUST JUNIPER-The First Adventure (Book 1)

The Mystery of the Mountain Lion Tracks(Book 2)

The Secret at the Lighthouse (Book 3)

Dolphins to the Rescue (Book 4)

Twin Trouble at Turtle Top (Book 5)

The Disappearing Snowman (Book 6)

Dog Day at The Deering Estate (Book 7)

The Royal Corgis (Book 8)

Barney's Big Surprise (Book 9)

Juniper in New York City (Book 10)

Lost in Wynwood (Book 11)

Mystery on the Natchez Trace (Book 12)

The Mystery of the Mountain Lion Tracks

A JUST JUNIPER Adventure

Written by Irene Hernández

Illustrated by Silvia María de la Fé

JUST JUNIPER Adventures

Book 2

JUST JUNIPER Adventures

justJuniperAdventures.com

Copyright © 2019 by Irene Hernández

The Library of Congress
Registration Number **TXu 2-136-279**
February 16, 2019
JUST JUNIPER Adventures- chapter book series

The Mystery of the Mountain Lion Tracks
A JUST JUNIPER Adventure

I dedicate this book to my second-grade students. They were my first listeners and critics...and of course to Juniper!

CONTENTS

Chapter 1   Grounded

Chapter 2   Not Again!

Chapter 3   The Expedition

Chapter 4   The Red Monkey

Chapter 5   Up on the Tree

Chapter 6   The Peanut Butter Jar

Chapter 7   The Footprints

Chapter 8   Crossing the Creek

Chapter 9   No Trespassing

Chapter 10   The Escape

Chapter 11   Cinnamon and Kiki

Chapter 12   Friends Forever

Chapter 1 – Grounded

I was sitting up on my bed thinking. Juniper was laying on the bed playing with her red monkey. I heard my cellphone go "ping".
I had a text.
"Sophie, can you finally come out of your room today?" Gaby texted me.
"Yes, finally!" I replied.
"Come over as soon as you can." Gaby wrote, *"we have to figure out what animal tried to come inside the cave."*
"Yes, I know. It was so scary!" I texted Gaby.
"Juniper, what do you think was making all those sounds outside the cave the other night?" I asked her.
Juniper jumped off the bed and looked at me.
"Woof! Woof!" She looked at me very seriously and barked. She jumped back up on the bed and cuddled next to me. I could feel her tremble.
"Juni, it's OK. We are safe now." I hugged her. She was still trembling. I talk to Juniper all the time. I know she is a dog,

but I know she understands everything I
say.
"Juniper let's go. We are going to Gaby's
house." I said getting up from the bed.
Juniper got up and wagged her tail. She
picked up her favorite toy, the red monkey
and ran to the door.

She held her head to one side and barked "Woof! Woof!" Juniper looked at me and I could almost hear her saying, "Can we really finally go out to play today?"

"Yes, Juni we can go outside today." I wrapped my arms around her. She licked my face. She is not a licker, but she was happy she was going outside!

We were grounded for two days. It had been just Juniper and me in my room for 48 hours. I was punished because I lied to my father. Dad was furious when he found out that Juniper and I had slept in the cave to hide the puppy from him.

"You are getting off easy!" He said when I told him the truth. "I should send you back to Miami right now!"

I cried for hours that day. I knew he was right. I should not have lied to him.

Mom and Dad are divorced. I live most of the year with Mom in Miami, but I spend my summer vacation and Christmas vacation with my father in North Carolina. I went down the stairs quietly. Juniper was quiet as a mouse. She did not want Dad getting mad at us again.

Dad was at the dining room table working on the laptop. He is a writer and spends lots of time writing.

"Dad, may I go to Gaby's house today?" I asked meekly.

Gaby is my best friend. We are both seven years old, almost eight. We are always together.

"Yes, Sophia, you may go to Gabriela's house today, but I want you back by 5 at the latest." I could tell that my father was still mad at me. He only calls me Sophia when he is upset with me. "You and Juniper better stay out of trouble."

"Of course, Dad, we will be back by 5 or even earlier." I promised him.

"Juni, bring me your leash" I called her.

Juniper put down the red monkey and picked up her pink leash. I noticed her collar was tight around her neck.

Juniper is a two-year-old Golden Retriever. She is very sweet and very big.

"Dad, I think we need to get Juniper a new collar, this one is getting too tight" I said.

"Yes, she is getting really, really big." Dad agreed "We'll get her a new collar tomorrow."

"That's good Dad, she really needs a new one."
Let's go get Gaby!" I called Juniper.
I could not wait to see my best friend, Gabriela. Juniper and I ran all the way to Gaby's house.
"Sophie, Juniper!" Gaby exclaimed and hugged us, "I missed you soooo much!"
"I missed you too." I told her.
"It was horrible, I thought I was never going to see you again!" Gaby continued, "I can't believe we could not even text or talk on the phone!"
Gaby is very dramatic.
We heard Ben calling us from down the hill. He was walking towards us. Aiden was walking with his younger brother and waving at us. Rocco was running next to them.
"Are your parents still mad at you?" Aiden asked.
"Yes" Gaby and I replied at the same time. Gaby had helped me hide Rocco, she slept in the cave with Juniper and me. Her parents punished her also.
"I can't stop thinking about the cave." Aiden said. "I still can't believe that a mountain lion tried to get inside."

"Let's go and try to figure it out!" Ben shouted as he ran ahead with Juniper, Rocco running at his heels.

We were walking behind them.
"Aiden, I've been thinking, I don't think the animal tracks we found around the cave are mountain lion tracks." I told him as we walked.
"Why?" he asked.
"My Dad says that there are no mountain lions in North Carolina." I replied seriously.
We were getting close to the cave.
"Oh no! I am scared already." Gaby shuddered remembering how scary it was the night we slept there.
"We are here!" Ben exclaimed, "I love this cave! It is the perfect clubhouse!"
The large refrigerator box we had used to cover the mouth of the cave was on the ground. Just seeing it send shivers down my spine. It had been so scary that night.
Ben climbed up on the rocks above the cave. Rocco was running behind Ben and barking.
Juniper just stood there. She was frozen staring at the cave.

Chapter 2 – Not Again!

"We have to find out what animal tried to come inside." I said standing next to Juniper.

"I think it was a mountain lion!" Ben yelled excitedly.

"Ben, you are just guessing," Gaby told him, "We have no idea."

"Let's go inside" Aiden agreed, "we may find more clues."

Gaby went inside the cave first. She ran out so fast that she knocked me down.

"Oh no! Not again!" Gaby screamed running outside.

"Gaby, what are you saying?" I asked, still sitting on a rock outside the cave.

"Look inside, Sophie!" She told me, her eyes wide open. Her body was shaking.

I got up and ran inside the cave. I could not believe my eyes!

Pieces of bread and potato chips were all over the floor. The plastic bags were ripped apart. The peanut butter jar was standing on the floor, unopened." What happened?" Ben asked excitedly.

"It came back!" I said terrified.

The four of us stood there looking at the mess on the floor. Juniper was standing close to me. She was shaking with fear.

Aiden kneeled on the floor to get a better look at the tracks.

"Sophie, why don't you think these are mountain lion tracks?" Aiden asked pointing at the tracks on the floor of the cave. "They look just like the picture of mountain lion tracks on my tablet" he continued as he showed me the pictures on the tablet.

"I am certain they are mountain lion tracks. They look exactly the same!" Ben exclaimed.

"They do look the same" I agreed, "but Dad told me there aren't any mountain lions left in North Carolina".

"Your Dad is right Sophie" Gaby said, "remember our teacher explained it to us in school last year."

Gaby and I go to the same school. We have been in the same class since kindergarten. Our moms are best friends and teach in the same school in Miami. We both speak English and Spanish because our mothers were born in Cuba. Actually, even Juniper is bilingual. She understands Spanish also because my grandma only speaks to her in Spanish.

"Are you sure?" asked Aiden.

"Yes, mountain lions are extinct from this area. Now they only live in the western United States." Gaby explained seriously.

"There are also some left in The Everglades. The Florida Panther is the same as a mountain lion." I told Aiden.

"I never knew that!" Ben yelled, standing on the rocks.

I was kneeling next to Aiden looking at the tracks.

"But Aiden, you are right, they do look exactly like mountain lion tracks. We must solve this mystery." I exclaimed.

Ben and Gaby knelt next to me. The four of us were kneeling on the floor looking for clues.

Juniper stood next to me. Her gaze fixed on the tracks also. A worried look on her face.

"Woof! Woof! Woof!" Juniper barked.

Rocco was oblivious.

He was playing with Juniper's red monkey.

Chapter 3 – The Expedition

"I'm really worried now, for it to happen one time is one thing, but it returned. This is serious. Maybe I should call Dad. He needs to see this." I said worriedly.

"Let's try to figure it out first. Let's go on a searching expedition" Aiden suggested, "Juniper can help us."

"Yes," I agreed with Aiden, "maybe we can find some clues before I tell Dad."

"Juniper come here." I called her. "Juni, you have to follow this scent" I told her as I held one of the plastic bags to her nose. Juni looked at me like I was crazy. She barked "Woof! Woof!"

"No way!" Juniper shook her head and looked at me. She barked again, "No way!" she was saying.

"Juniper is still afraid. She remembers how scared we were the night we slept in the cave" I told Aiden. "She does not want anything to do with a mountain lion."

"Juniper, nothing is going to happen. We are just going on an expedition looking for clues." Aiden reassured her.

"Juni is too smart! She doesn't want to go! I don't want to go either!" Gaby exclaimed, "I'm scared too!"

"You don't have to be afraid Gaby," I reassured her, "most wild animals will not come out during the day, only at night."

"We said it can't be a mountain lion!" Gaby said terrified, "Who knows what the heck it is?!"

"I want to go on a mountain lion hunt." Ben said. "I am sure it is a mountain lion!"

"Ben, we are not hunting for anything!" Aiden told Ben seriously, "We are just looking for clues."

"Rocco, you are brave. You follow the scent." Ben held the plastic bag to the puppy's nose. "Let's go!"

Rocco took a whiff. He ran right over and started eating the pieces of bread that were left on the ground.

"No Rocco!" Ben exclaimed. "No!"

Rocco looked at us as if saying, "isn't this what you want me to do?"

We all burst out laughing. We could not stop. The puppy ate every piece of bread and all the potato chips left on the floor of the cave.

"Juniper, please follow the scent." I begged her as I hugged her.

Juni looked at me seriously. She went over to smell the plastic bag.

"Woof! Woof!" Juni barked as she ran out of the cave. "Follow me!" I knew she was saying.

We ran after her. Juniper was going fast. She was running down the hill through the forest. She got to a tree. She looked up and stopped.

"Why are you stopping here, Juniper?" I asked her.

She kept looking up at the tree and barking. We were all looking up to see if we could see anything.

"There's nothing up there Juni" I said, "it's just a tree!"

She ran to the other side of the tree and came back with a banana peel in her mouth.

"Is that a banana peel?" Asked Gaby, "that doesn't make any sense."

"What's a banana peel doing in the middle of the woods?" Gaby continued.

Juniper kept nudging at me. She kept trying to give me the banana peel.

"Yes, Juniper, finding a banana peel here is very strange." I told her, "But that is not what we are looking for."
Juniper dropped the banana peel on the floor and looked disappointed.
"Here, smell this again." Aiden took the plastic bag and held it under Juniper's nose again "Follow the scent, Juniper. You can do it!"

Juni did not move. She picked up the banana peel again. She barked "Woof! Woof! Woof!"

"OK, Juniper, this banana peel must be important." I told her as I petted her. "Did the mountain lion pick it up?" I asked her. Juni dropped the banana peel and got up on her hind legs to kiss me. She licked my face, and I knew she was happy I understood her.

"Aiden, I think the mountain lion or whatever animal picked up this banana peel" I said, "that's why she keeps giving it to me!"

"Of course, that's why Juniper keeps insisting," Aiden agreed.

Juni kept looking at the banana peel. She seemed confused. Then she started running again.

We were deep in the forest when the thunder started. The sky was dark.

"We better go back. There is a bad storm coming." Aiden said.

"Yes, I have to get back home." Gaby said, "I don't want to get grounded again!"

The rain was starting to come down.

"We can meet tomorrow morning at the cave" Gaby said as we all ran in the direction of our houses.

"Yes, we'll come up with a plan of action tomorrow." Aiden said running home. "Hurry up Rocco! Hurry Ben!"

"Come on Juni! Let's get home before the storm!" I called.

Chapter 4 – The Red Monkey

We were soaked by the time we got home. The storm got stronger and stronger. It continued all night. The rain and thundering would not stop. Juniper did not let me sleep. She kept waking me up all night. Juniper does not like thunder and to make matters worse she could not find her red monkey.

"Juni, don't worry" I kept telling her, "I am sure you left the red monkey in the cave."
Juniper looked at me with a terrified look in her eyes.
"We will get up early and go find him." I promised her.

Juniper was up at the crack of dawn. She was licking my face trying to wake me up. This was not like her at all. Juniper is usually a sleepy head. I always have to wake her up.

"Juni, it's too early!" I told her looking at the time on my phone, "it's only 7AM!

She went to the closet and brought me one of my hiking boots.

"Let's go find my red monkey!" Her eyes were begging me.

"Juni, it is much too early." I told her again as I got dressed. She barked, pushed open the bedroom door, and went down the stairs. She stood by the front door waiting for me. Juni is very sweet, but she can be very stubborn when she wants something.

"OK Juniper, we'll go find your red monkey" I told her, "But first I have to write Dad a note, so he knows where we are. We don't want him to get mad at us again."

Dad,

Juniper and I went to the cave. Juniper left her red monkey in the cave, and she is driving me crazy.

Love you,

Sophie

I left the note on the kitchen counter by the coffee pot. Dad would see it when he got up.

I went outside.

I am always surprised how chilly the mornings are in the mountains. My Dad always says that it feels chilly to me because I am a Miami girl. It's never cold in Miami.
Juniper ran all the way down the hill.

When I caught up with her, she was acting crazy. Running in circles around the cave.

The red monkey was nowhcre to be found. Juniper kept sniffing and looking up at me. I searched inside the cave.

The only thing I saw was the peanut butter jar on the floor and a small cardboard box with a blue flannel shirt and a tennis ball. The red monkey was not there.

"Juni, don't worry, we'll find him," I tried to sound convincing.

Suddenly Juniper barked and ran into the woods. I ran after her.

"Juni, please wait! Don't leave me behind!" I begged as I ran after her.

Juniper ignored me and kept running. She did not stop until she got to the tree where she had found the banana peel the day before. Juniper got on her hind legs and started scratching the trunk of the tree. She kept looking up and barking.

The red monkey was high up on one of the branches!

Juniper laid down on the ground and started whimpering.
"Juni, don't worry" I hugged her, "I promise we will get your red monkey down from the tree."
Who took the red monkey from the cave? How did it get up on the tree?

Chapter 5 – Up on the Tree

"Help!" I texted Gaby, *"Come meet me at the cave!"*

"Right now?" she texted right back, *"I'm still in bed. Why? What happened?"*

"Yes, right now. Please come." I replied, *"You'll see when you get here."*

"I'll be there in a flash." Gaby answered.

"Good," I texted her, *"Hurry!"*

I sat down next to Juniper. She was still whimpering and looking up at the red monkey on the high branch of the tree.

"Juni, let's go to the cave." I hugged her. "Gaby is coming over to help us get your monkey down from the tree."

Juniper got up and started walking with me. Every few minutes she would look back at the tree and whimper.

"Sophie! Juniper! Where are you?" We heard Gaby calling us as we got near the cave.

Gaby got there very fast.

"Here Gaby, we are here!" I called back, waving to her.

"What happened?" Gaby asked, "why are you here so early?"

"Come follow us. You won't believe this!" I told her.

Juniper led the way. When we got to the tree she looked up and barked.

"We were here yesterday" Gaby said.

"Yes," I agreed, "Look up!" I said pointing at the branches.

"What?! How did Juniper's red monkey get up there?!" Gaby screamed.

"I have no idea." I said hugging Juniper.

"How are we going to get it?" Gaby asked, "it's too high."

I had an idea, "Maybe we can throw a ball up and knock it down."

Juniper got up and started running.

"Juniper, where are you going now?" I ran after her.

"Sophie, how do you think it got up on the tree?!" Gaby's eyes were wide open as she ran after Juniper and me.

Juniper did not stop running until she got to the cave.

Juniper went inside and got the tennis ball we had left in the box the night we slept there to hide the puppy from Dad.

"Good girl!" I told her, "Juni, we'll throw the tennis ball up and knock down your monkey from the tree."

We ran back to the tree.

"Juni, give me the ball, I'll get your monkey!" I said taking the ball from her mouth.

I threw the tennis ball up in the air. I missed by a mile!

"I'll try again! I'll get it this time! I exclaimed.

I tried again. I missed the branch again.

I must have thrown the ball up ten times!

Juniper kept looking at me very seriously. She wanted her red monkey. At first she was just looking at me and whimpering.

"Woof! Woof! Woof!" Juni was getting desperate.

"Let me try," Gaby said, "maybe I can do
it."

Gaby threw the ball up and hit the branch. "Yes!" I said, "Gaby, try again!"

Gaby kept hitting the branch, but the red monkey would not move.

Juniper stood there anxiously waiting for the red monkey.

"Juni, don't worry. We'll get your monkey." I held her face in my hands and kissed her.
"I don't think the tennis ball is heavy enough." I told Gaby.
"Do you think Ben and Aiden have a football?" Gaby asked.
"Woof! Woof!" Juniper barked and licked Gaby's face. Juniper liked Gaby's idea.
"Gaby, that's brilliant!" I told her as I took out my phone, "I will text Aiden right now."

"Do you have a football?" I texted Aiden.
"Yes, I do," he replied.
"Please bring it to the cave." I asked him.
"Right now?" Aiden asked me.

"Yes, as soon as you can," I replied.
"We'll be there in five minutes." He wrote back.
"Good!" I said, *"see you soon."*
"Juni, Gaby, let's go to the cave, Aiden is bringing a football."

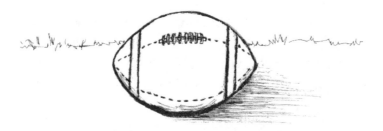

I could tell Juni was still upset about her red monkey.
We started walking towards the cave.
"Sophie, how did the monkey get up there?" Gaby asked.
"Gaby, this is getting stranger and stranger" I said, "I don't think a mountain lion or whatever can climb that high!"
"Yes, it is just too weird!" Gaby agreed.
We sat on the rocks outside the cave waiting for Aiden to bring the football. Juniper was sitting next to me. I knew she was sad.

Suddenly Juniper got up and barked, "Woof! Woof! Woof!" Juniper heard Ben and Aiden coming.

"Are we going to play football this early?" Ben was running up the hill and calling out, "that's not fair, I can't play with this cast on my arm!"

"No, Ben we need the football to get Juniper's red monkey down from the tree," I told him when they got to the cave.

"What tree?" Aiden asked.

"Follow us," I said, "you won't believe this."

Juniper was already running through the forest. She was taking us to the tree. Rocco was barking and trying to catch up to her.

"How in the world did Juniper's monkey get up on that tree?!" Aiden exclaimed when he saw the red monkey.

"It was the mountain lion!" Ben screamed. Juniper looked at Ben in disbelief. "Woof! Woof! Woof!" She sounded worried.

"Juni, don't worry," I hugged her, "Aiden will get your red monkey."

He threw the football up. Aiden missed the branch completely. He tried a few times, but he kept missing.

"Let me try," Gaby said, "I almost got it with the tennis ball."

Gaby threw the football and hit the branch on her first try!

The red monkey came flying down.

"Yes, Gaby you did it!" I screamed.
Juniper was watching the red monkey fall.
She jumped and caught it in midair!

Chapter 6 – The Peanut Butter Jar

"Juni, are you happy now?" I hugged her, "that was a great catch."
"Yes Juniper, what a fantastic catch!" Gaby told Juni, petting her.

We were walking back home. I could tell that Juniper was exhausted from the ordeal. All she wanted was to be home with her monkey.

"Aiden, do you think a mountain lion can climb that high?" I asked, "why would it take the red monkey up the tree?"
"Beats me, I don't understand anything anymore!" Aiden replied.
"It doesn't make any sense." Gaby agreed.
"I am sure it was the mountain lion," exclaimed Ben, "they are cats so they can climb trees."
"Yes Ben, you are right. They are cats and they do climb." Aiden said seriously.
"I'm starving!" Gaby said, "I didn't even have breakfast!"
"We didn't have breakfast either." Ben said, "I'm starving too!"

"Let's go home and try to and figure this out." I said, "My Dad makes the best grilled cheese sandwiches."

"Yes, he does! They are awesome." Gaby was always hungry.

I took out my phone to text Dad. I knew he was going to like that my friends were going over to eat his grilled cheese sandwiches.

"Dad, can you make grilled cheese sandwiches?" I texted him.

"Of course! How many?" He asked, "are you coming over right now?"

"Four sandwiches, and yes we are on our way there now." I answered.

Juniper was looking at me and looking at Rocco, "only four?" She seemed worried.

"Juni, you know Dad will make enough sandwiches to give you and Rocco some," I told her, "He likes to give you treats."

She wagged her tail and started running ahead. She held her red monkey securely in her mouth.

When we got home, Juniper went straight to my bedroom. She put the red monkey in the wicker basket where she keeps all her toys. She knew the red monkey was safe there.

"This is the best grilled cheese sandwich I have ever tasted!" Ben said.

"I told you they were awesome." Gaby replied.

"Dad, are there mountain lions here?" I asked when we finished having lunch.

"Sophia, there are not supposed to be any mountain lions left here in North Carolina," Dad replied, "but Bob swears he saw one a few nights ago, I don't believe him, but he is sure he saw one."

"Who's Bob?" Ben asked.

"Bob is our neighbor. He lives three houses down the road." Dad explained.

"Dad, is that possible?" I asked.

"Anything is possible!" Ben replied.

"Yes Ben, anything is possible" my father explained, "but it is not likely."

"Sophia, why are you asking?" Dad continued.

"Just curious," I replied looking seriously at Ben, trying to get him to stop talking.

Aiden realized his brother was going to keep asking questions and called him, "Ben, bring me your plate, help me clear the table."

Ben continued "We don't know how the red monkey got up on the tree ..."
Ben was still talking to Dad.
Suddenly Juniper ran to Ben, she knocked him down on the floor and started licking his face.
"Juniper, that tickles!" Ben was rolling on the floor and laughing." that really tickles!" Juni kept on licking him until he forgot all about the mountain lion.

That's Juni for you! She always saves the day!

"Let's go back to the cave," I wanted to get Ben out of the house before he told Dad about the mountain lion tracks.
"Yes, let's go Ben, let's go Rocco," Gaby realized what I was trying to do, "thanks for the sandwiches. They were awesome." Gaby told my dad.
"Come on Ben," Aiden said dragging his brother out of the house before Ben put his foot in his mouth. Ben was about to tell Dad about the tracks and the red monkey up on the tree. "The sandwiches were very good. Thank you." Aiden thanked Dad as he walked out the door with Ben.

"Glad you liked them." Dad replied.

"Dad, I will be back by 4 o'clock. Is that, OK?" I asked.

"Yes Sophie, 4 o'clock is fine, remember we need to go get groceries today and get Juniper her new leash." he reminded me. We started walking towards the cave. Juniper was looking at me with a knowing look on her face. "See what I did?" She was asking me.

"Yes Juniper, you are amazing! I know exactly what you did!" I told her as I kissed her, "you stopped Ben from telling Dad about the mountain lion!"

Juniper nodded "yes" and wagged her tail. She had a smug look on her face.

Aiden came over and petted her, "Juniper you are a genius!"

"She is Just Juniper!" I said, "and she is just perfect!"

Gaby, Ben and Rocco were walking ahead. They got to the cave before us.

"Oh no! Oh no! Not again!" I heard Gaby screaming.

I ran into the cave. Juniper and Aiden followed me.

 The peanut butter jar was on the floor. It was opened and half empty.

"How is this even possible?!" I exclaimed.
"I don't understand," muttered Aiden.
"I told you so!" Ben reminded us, "anything is possible!"
We looked around. The mountain lion tracks were all over the cave again.
"There is no way a mountain lion can open a jar of peanut butter!" Gaby was freaking out, "maybe it can climb a tree, but it can't do this!"
We stood there frozen, staring at the half empty jar on the floor!

Chapter 7 – The Footprints

"Sophie, look at the jar of peanut butter. Who opened it?" Gaby asked me, her eyes popping out, "this is getting crazier and crazier!"

"Yes, it is too weird." I agreed, "who ate the peanut butter?"

"Come over here. Look what I found." Ben called us, "look at these footprints!" He yelled as he took off his shoe. "I think they are exactly the same size as my foot."

"What footprints?" Asked Gaby, running over to Ben.

"Wait Ben! Don't mess up those footprints!" Aiden ran and pushed Ben aside.

I went over to look at the ground. Next to the mountain lion tracks there were two

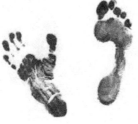

footprints. "Ben is right. These footprints are about the same size as his feet!" I exclaimed.

Ben had taken off his shoes and was standing barefoot next to the footprints.

"They are the same size, but they look very, very different." Gaby was kneeling on the floor examining the footprints. "Sophie, come look."

"These are very weird footprints." I said, "these little toes are long, and the big toe is very thin and very far apart from the other toes." I was kneeling on the floor. Juniper was next to me. She was sniffing all around the footprints.

"Woof! Woof! Woof!" Juniper barked and ran out of the cave.

"Juniper, wait for us!" I called her as we ran after her. She ignored me and kept running. "Juni, slow down!" She was running through the trees at full speed. She stopped when she got to the tree where we had found the red monkey. Juniper was sniffing all around. She found the banana peel on the floor. She picked it up and brought it to me."

"What, Juni, what?" I asked her. "Why are you giving me the banana peel again?"

"Woof! Woof!" Juniper looked up at the tree, "Woof! Woof!"

"Oh no!" Gaby exclaimed, "look what I found."

Gaby was pointing at the lid of the peanut butter jar laying on the ground.

"How did it get this far from the cave?" I wondered.

"This is very strange," Aiden was kneeling on the floor. "The weird footprints are here again but the mountain lion tracks are here too!"

Ben was jumping up and down, "I told you anything is possible!" He exclaimed.

Juniper was looking up at the tree and barking.

She picked up the banana peel again. She got up on her hind legs and was scratching the trunk of the tree.

"Juni, what is it? What are you trying to tell me?" I went over and petted her.

Aiden was looking at pictures of footprints on the tablet. "Come look at this!" He called us. He was pointing at the pictures of two sets of footprints.

"These are chimpanzee footprints!" He yelled.

"Unbelievable!" He said showing us the picture of children footprints next to the picture of the chimp's footprint on the tablet. "These pictures could have been taken from the ground of the cave!" Aiden exclaimed.

"Chimpanzee footprints?" Gaby's jaw dropped.

"A chimpanzee in the woods, in the mountains of North Carolina?" I said seriously, "that's impossible."

"A chimpanzee and a mountain lion! This is great!" Ben said. He was thrilled. "I told you so. I told you so! Anything is possible!"

"Monkeys love bananas." Aiden said, "that's what Juniper was trying to tell us."

"Yes," I exclaimed, "Juni you are so smart, you were right all the time. The banana peel is a very important clue in this mystery. The chimpanzee must have dropped it.

Juni wagged her tail and started licking my face. She was happy I finally understood.

"You are just too smart!" I hugged and petted her.

"Now we have mountain lion tracks and chimpanzee footprints." Gaby's eyes were wide open. "What the heck is going on?"

"Sophie, this is very strange." Aiden agreed. "I think we need to follow these tracks to see where they lead us."

We were at the edge of the forest; we could see a creek not far from us.

"Aiden, we have never gone beyond the creek. Dad warned me never to go beyond the creek alone." I said looking at the small creek just a few feet away.

"You are not alone now." Ben interrupted, "there are four of us and two dogs!"

"Ben is right Sophie. You are not alone." Gaby said her voice trembling, "we need to get to the bottom of this mystery."

Gaby was trying hard to be brave.

"I guess we have to. We really have to solve this mystery." I said as I looked at the small creek again.

"Come on Juni, let's go across the creek." I called Juniper.

Juniper just stood there. She was looking at the creek with a very serious look on her face.

"Woof! Woof!" Juniper barked but did not move.

Chapter 8 – Crossing the Creek

"The water is very cold!" Gaby called out as she put her foot in the creek. "I'm going to try to step on the rocks, so I don't get wet." She said, "these are brand new clothes, I don't want to get all stinky!"

That's Gaby for you. Always dainty and neat.

"I love the cold water. I'm wading across." Ben had taken off his shoes and was knee deep in water. "Rocco, come here boy!"

"Oh! Oh! This is freezing!" Ben screamed excitedly.

"Ben be careful. Don't get your cast wet." Aiden reminded him.

"Don't worry Aiden. I will hold my arm above my head," Ben replied holding his broken arm above his head.

"Juni, let's go across the creek." I called her as I took of my shoes.

I put one foot in the water and jumped right out.

"It's too cold. I can't go in." I said trying to climb on the rocks like Gaby.

Juniper kept looking at me with a worried look in her eyes. She wasn't moving. She barked and looked in the direction of the house.

"Juni, I know Dad said not to go beyond the creek, but it is safe. We are not alone." I reassured her, "Dad won't be mad."

Juniper loves water but she is a very good dog. She really did not want to disobey Dad, so she just stood there. I was going to have to convince Juniper to jump in the water.

"Juni, jump in! This is so much fun!" I called her as I braced myself and jumped in the freezing water. The water was so cold that my skin tingled. I could not even feel my toes! "Come in Juniper! You love swimming. You go swimming in Miami all the time." I reminded her, throwing water and splashing her.

Juniper finally jumped in the creek. She looked at me with her eyes wide open and ran out of the water immediately. "Woof! Woof!" She kept looking at me. I knew she was telling me "You are crazy! This is not like Miami at all! It is cold!" Juniper was shivering.

"Juni, come back in. It is only cold for a few seconds." I coaxed her. "It's fun! You just have to get used to it!" I kept splashing water on her hoping to convince her.

"Juniper, look at Rocco," Ben said, "he is only a puppy, and he is not afraid."

"Woof! Woof! Woof!" Rocco called Juniper.

I guess seeing Rocco having so much fun did the trick. Juniper jumped in the creek again. Soon she forgot all about the cold water and she forgot all about Dad. I knew she would love the creek once she started playing. Juni loves water.

"Juni, for someone who didn't want to come in the water you sure made a splash!" I told her as I hugged her. "Now you look like you are swimming in the ocean in Miami."

"Juni, be careful, there are rocks here." I had to remind her; she was so excited that I was afraid she was going to get hurt.

"Ben, be careful with the rocks." Aiden kept reminding his brother, "they are slippery."

We spent a long-time swimming in the creek. It was cold but we got used to it. It was fun. We even forgot about the mountain lion. We tried to convince Gaby to come in the water, but she did not believe in getting wet and messy.

Gaby managed to stay dry jumping from rock to rock.

"Don't worry about me." Gaby said when she got to the other side. "I will just sit here and get a suntan."

That was just so Gaby!

When we finally got out of the creek we were shivering. I laid down on a rock next to Gaby.

"The sun feels wonderful." I said, "I have to dry out a bit. We are soaked." "Yes, it's good that it is hot and sunny now. Let's try to dry out before we continue" Aiden commented twisting his dripping t-shirt as he sat on the rock next to me. We had barely sat down and gotten comfortable when Juniper took off like a maniac.

"Juniper, Stop!" I yelled. "Where are you going now?" I asked.

Juni looked back at me, "Woof, Woof!" She kept on running.

Ben and Rocco were trying to catch up to Juniper. We started running behind them. "Hey! Look at the big fence over there!" Juniper got to the fence and was sniffing around. "Woof! Woof! Woof!" She barked excitedly.

The fence was very high. It was about seven feet tall with barbed wire on the top. All along the fence there were big cardboard signs with "DANGER" and "NO TRESPASSING" written on them.

Chapter 9 – NO TRESPASSING!

"I want to go home." Gaby stammered looking at the fence. "I don't like all those "DANGER" signs!"

"Woof! Woof!" Juniper barked and went over to where Gaby was standing. Juni wanted to go back home also.

"Gaby, you were the one who convinced me to cross the creek and follow the tracks." I said, "you can't get cold feet now."
"Don't be afraid Juni, I'll take care of you." I hugged and petted Juniper.
Aiden and Ben were staring at all the signs on the fence.
"Sophie, who lives here?" Aiden asked me.
"I have no idea," I said, "but it looks very scary. They sure don't want anyone going inside!"
"Let's just walk around the perimeter," Aiden suggested, "let's see if we can see anything."
We were all walking around the fenced area. It was dense with trees.

"It looks like a forest in there," commented Ben, "It looks weird. I have never seen so many trees fenced in."

Suddenly we heard "Grrrr! Grrrr! Grrrr! We froze.
"Sophie, what was that?" Gaby hugged me. Juniper ran to my side and almost knocked me down.
"Grrrrr! Grrrrr! Grrrr!"

We heard the sound again.
"Let's go home," Gaby exclaimed, "I'm scared!"
"Grrrr! Grrrr!"
Suddenly a mountain lion appeared on the other side of the fence. It was staring at us and growling.
"Look!" I screamed terrified. "It is a real mountain lion!"
The six of us became statues. We were afraid to move. I think we were afraid to breathe. We stood in a trance staring at the mountain lion. The mountain lion was staring back at us.
Suddenly we saw very tall lady with long red hair walking towards us. "Stay right

where you are!" she yelled at us. "What are you kids doing here?"

"Grrrr! Grrrr!" growled the mountain lion.

"What the heck?!" Ben screamed, "What's that lady doing in there with the mountain lion?"

"Oh no!" Gaby yelled holding on to me for dear life.

Juniper was standing in front of us trying to act brave.

"Grrrr! Grrrr!"

The mountain lion was still staring at us and growling.

"Come here Cinnamon!" the tall red-haired lady was calling the mountain lion "Stop growling right now!"

The tall lady kept walking towards us. "Cinnamon, stop growling!" She said as she held the mountain lion and put her on a leash.

The mountain lion stopped growling but kept staring at us.

"Let me ask you one more time, what are you kids doing here?" The lady was looking at us sternly. "Where do you live?" She asked, holding the mountain lion close to her.

"We live on the other side of the creek" I stammered still staring at the mountain lion.

Suddenly out of nowhere we heard "Haoooo! Haoooo! Haoooo!"

A chimpanzee flew out of the trees. The chimp landed gingerly on the mountain lions back. The chimpanzee looked at us and took a bow!

We were dumbfounded.

"We were right!" Ben screamed, "a mountain lion and a chimp!" Ben was jumping up and down, "I knew it was possible! Anything is possible!"

Ch

"Kiki stop clowning around! This is serious!" The red-haired lady was speaking to the chimpanzee now. "That was a very good landing, but you have to be careful. You can hurt Cinnamon's back."

Kiki shook her head saying no. She got off of Cinnamon's back and hugged and kissed the mountain lion. She was telling the lady she loved Cinnamon and would not hurt her!

"Kiki, I know you love Cinnamon, and you will not hurt her on purpose, but you still have to be careful." The lady was petting Cinnamon now. "Good girl Cinnamon. I like how you stopped growling." She told Cinnamon as she took out a treat from her pocket and gave it to the mountain lion.

"The mountain lion looks just like a Florida Panther" I whispered in Gaby's ear.

"Yes." Gaby whispered nervously.

We were still standing there speechless. We were fascinated by Cinnamon and Kiki.

I could not believe my eyes. This was the most exciting thing that had ever happened to me.

"OK, let's start this again. Exactly, what are you kids doing here?" The tall lady asked us. She sounded mad.

"We live on the other side of the creek," I answered, "we were following the mountain lion tracks and the footprints."

"What do you mean you were following the tracks?" The red-haired lady looked at me sternly, "that's impossible Cinnamon and Kiki have never been outside this fence."

"Yes, they have!" Ben exclaimed. "They go to our cave all the time!"

"They go to your cave?" The lady asked, "What do you mean they go to your cave?"

"Yes, Ben is right," I explained, "the first night that they went to our cave they really scared us." I continued, "Gaby, Juniper and I were sleeping in the cave hiding Rocco from my dad." I said trying to explain to the red-haired lady. "Cinnamon really scared us. She was growling and trying to come inside the cave."

"Hold on a second," the tall red-haired lady asked, "and what did you think you were doing sleeping in a cave?" She continued, "whose bright idea was that? And what do you mean by 'the first time'? How any times have Cinnamon and Kiki escaped?"

"It's a long story," I sighed. I did not want to remember how angry my father had been when he found out we had slept in the cave.

"We don't know how many times," Ben replied, "but one time they ate the bread and the peanut butter, and they took Juniper's red monkey."

Juniper barked loudly, "Woof, Woof, Woof!" when she remembered her red monkey.

"We knew it was a mountain lion and a chimpanzee by their tracks," continued Aiden, "I looked them up on my tablet."

"This is very serious," the lady said looking at Kiki and then at Cinnamon. "Kiki, is this true? Did you figure out a way to get out?"

The chimpanzee covered her face with her hands and looked down to the floor.

"This is awesome! Kiki admits she is guilty. She understands you!" Ben was thrilled.

We were all amazed.

"Kiki look at me!" The lady was very upset now.

The chimpanzee uncovered her eyes and looked up at the red-haired lady.

"Kiki, do you remember what happened to you when you escaped from the Everglades Wild Animal Rescue in Miami?" She was looking sternly at Kiki and waiting for an answer.

Kiki covered her eyes again and shook her head up and down. She was saying "Yes, I remember."

The red-haired lady was furious, "I thought you had learned your lesson!"

The lady continued, "and you even convinced Cinnamon to go with you?"

Now Kiki dropped down to the floor and covered her whole body with her hands. Cinnamon went over and laid down next to her.

"They are too cute!" Gaby squealed in delight.

"Yes, so cute and so smart!" I agreed.

"There is nothing cute about this!" The lady was looking at Kiki and Cinnamon, "it could have been very serious. You could have been shot and killed. We could have lost our license for the Smoky Mountains Wild Animal Rescue."

"I will deal with the two of you later!" She told Cinnamon and Kiki.

"Do your parents know what you kids are up to?" She was looking directly at me and Juniper now.

"Young lady, I see you have a phone in your pocket, call your mother right now. I need to speak to her." She told me.

"My mother lives in Miami but I can call her right now." I said hoping I could get away with it. I much rather she spoke to my mother in Miami, than to Dad here. I thought to myself.

She looked at me very seriously, "Who do you live with here in the mountains?"

"My Dad" I replied.

"Call him." She put her hand by the fence waiting for me to call my father and hand her the phone.

I could feel Juniper trembling and heard her whimpering next to me. She knew we were in big trouble!

Dad picked up on the first ring. "Sophie, where are you?" Dad asked me, "remember I told you to be back by four. It is four-fifteen already. We must go do groceries."

"Dad, we have a small problem," I tried to sound normal, "a lady wants to speak to you."

"Sophia, what do you mean 'a small problem'? Put the lady on the phone right now" Dad knew something was wrong.
I handed my cellphone to the lady.

"Hello, my name is Alice Baxter. Your daughter and her friends are here with me." She was very serious. "I think it is best that you come pick them up and we talk about this face to face."
The tall red-haired lady was listening to my father on the phone, "Yes, come over right now," she continued, "my husband and I just opened The Smoky Mountains Wild Animal Rescue. We are right off Laurel Hill Road. Make a left, and drive about half a mile on the dirt road. I will meet you at the gate."
"Your father is coming right over," she said to me. "you kids continue walking on the outside of the fence until you get to the gate. I will meet you there."

We were all silent as we walked to the gate.

It felt like we were going to face a firing squad.

Juniper kept whimpering. Rocco was the only one playing around. He had no clue!

It must be nice being a puppy, I thought.

Juniper was afraid, she would not stop whimpering. "Juniper, it's all right," I hugged her. "It's not your fault. You were right. We should not have crossed the creek.

Chapter 11– Cinnamon and Kiki

"There's the entrance" Aiden said pointing to the gate. The Smoky Mountain Wild Animal Rescue was written on a sign on the fence next to the gate. "No Trespassing" signs were all over the fence. We stood by the gate waiting for Alice Baxter.

Soon we saw her walking towards the gate. She was alone. The animals were not with her.

"You better wait outside until your father gets here." She said, "I don't want him upset that you are inside where we have wild animals."

"They are not wild." Ben exclaimed.

"They are wild animals. They happen to be tame because we brought them up since they were very young," she explained, "but they are wild animals."

"How did you get them when they were babies?" I asked.

"Cinnamon's mother was shot in the Everglades by a poacher. She was rescued with her sister Ginger by a park ranger."

"You are from Miami?" Gaby asked incredulously.

"She is a Florida Panther!" I exclaimed, "I just knew it! She is beautiful. Florida Panthers are my favorite wild animals."

The tall red-haired lady continued, "Ginger and Cinnamon were only four weeks old when the ranger found them. He brought them to us at the Everglades Wild Animal Rescue. Ginger did not survive." She said sadly, "we bottle fed Cinnamon until she was strong enough to eat on her own. Our goal at the refuges is always to nurse the animals back to health and reintroduce them to their natural habitat."

The six of us stood there fascinated. Even Rocco was listening to Alice tell the story of how they got Cinnamon.

"We are from Miami also," Gaby interrupted her. "We come here for summer vacation and Christmas vacation."

"Yes, we are from Miami," Alice replied, "we have run The Everglades Wild Animal Rescue for 25 years. My son runs it now. We just opened The Smoky Mountain Wild Animal Rescue last month." She explained.

"How did you get Kiki?" Gaby asked her.

"Kiki belonged to a circus that came to Miami. They were trying to train her to do circus tricks, but she was very mischievous. The owner beat her with a stick to get her to behave."

"Oh no!" We all said in unison.

"Someone from the circus reported it to Animal Cruelty and they brought her to us. She was only six months old. She was adorable but quite a handful!" Alice continued, "she is still a handful!"

"Yes, she is! She escaped with Cinnamon!" I agreed with Alice. "They really, really scared us the first night when we were sleeping in the cave!"

"Where are Kiki and Cinnamon now?" Aiden asked.

"They are both punished." Alice was upset, "they should know better, and so should you." She told the four of us.

"I am sure we are going to be punished also." I assured her, "wait till my father finds out."

"Do you kids realize how dangerous it was to follow wild animal tracks?" Alice was very serious now, "do you realize you could have been attacked and killed?"

My Dad was driving up in his truck on the dirt road. Juniper went up to Alice and started licking her hand.

Juniper is not a licker, but she was all over Alice. She stood on her hind legs and was trying to lick Alice's face, but Alice was too tall.

"What's her name?" Alice asked, "she is one smart dog, she is trying to soften me up before I talk to your dad!" She was petting Juniper and laughing.

"Her name is Juniper." I answered.

"Juniper, you win!" Alice told her, "It really was all Kiki's fault. I will talk to your dad, but I will make sure that he knows that Kiki and Cinnamon are the ones to blame for what happened."

"Thanks, you are sooo nice!" Gaby told her.

"Thank your dog!" She said laughing and petting Juniper again.

Alice walked over to the truck and started talking to Dad. I could tell by the expression on his face that he was not too mad. He was smiling.

What a relief! I thought.

I went over to Juniper and kissed her a million times. "Thank you, Juni, you saved my life again." I told her.

"Juniper always saves the day!" Gaby said proudly. "She is brilliant!"

"She is a genius!" Ben said.

Juniper looked at us very seriously, "I'm Just Juniper." she was reminding us again.

Alice Baxter and Dad were walking towards us.

"Do you want to come inside to meet Cinnamon and Kiki?" Alice was asking Dad.

"I would love to." Dad said.

"Cinnamon and Kiki are punished. They must remain in their cages today, but you are welcome to come in." She continued, "are you kids thirsty? That was a long hike. Come in and have something to drink."

"Sophia, we will talk about this later." Dad said, "you know I told you never to go beyond the creek."

"I know Dad, I'm sorry," I replied.

"Come on in," Alice said as she opened the front door, "Cinnamon and Kiki are in their room."

"They live inside?!" Gaby asked, her eyes were wide open.

"Yes, they are free to roam around the house or go outside. We never thought they would leave the grounds." Alice explained.

We followed Alice past the kitchen to the back of the house. There was a big, enclosed porch with two cages. Cinnamon was in one crate and Kiki was in the other. The minute they saw us they got up. They were very curious.

"This is Cinnamon," Alice walked over to the cage.

"I can see why you called her Cinnamon," Dad commented. "She is exactly the color of cinnamon; she is very beautiful."

"Yes, her sister Ginger had more orange in her coat, but she was just as beautiful. It's a pity we could not save her." She said sadly, "my husband did all he could, but we lost her."

"Is your husband Dr. Dan Baxter?" Dad asked, "is he the vet from Miami who just started working at Admiral's Pet Adoption Center?"

"Yes, how do you know of him?" Alice asked.

"My good friends Liz and Viv are volunteers at Admirals. They were telling me what a nice guy Dan is," Dad explained, "it's a small world. They were telling me all about your work rescuing animals and nursing them back to health until they can be released back into the wild."

"Yes, that is our life long work, first in Florida and now here." Alice walked over to the other cage and said, " This is Kiki. We love her but she is turning my red hair white!"

Kiki looked down and covered her face again.

We all started laughing. She was too cute.

"Kiki, it is not funny at all! Just wait until Dan finds out. He is going to be very upset with you." Alice was looking seriously at Kiki.

Kiki started going "Boo, Boo, Boo, Boo" and making a crying face.

We were about to burst out laughing when Alice stopped us.

"Do not laugh at her! Kiki needs to know that what she did was very wrong." Alice said. "What are your names?" She asked us, "I know she is Juniper, and he is

Rocco. Come here Juniper, come here Rocco come get a treat" she called them.

"I'm Sophie, and this is my best friend Gaby," I said pointing, "and these are Aiden and Ben, they are brothers."

"I am very happy to meet you, even if it was not under the best circumstances" Alice continued, "Dan and I love to have kids come over."

"Can we play with Kiki and Cinnamon?" I asked.

"Not today because they are punished." Alice explained, "but if your parents allow it, and only with both Dan and me present, then yes, you can play with Kiki and Cinnamon another day.

"Awesome!" Ben exclaimed. "I'm sure grandma will let us."

"Daddy?"I asked, looking at him hopefully.

"Yes Sophie, it will be fine as long as I am here, and Alice or Dan are present.

"Thank you, Dad,"

I ran over and kissed him and hugged him hard, "I love you, Daddy!"

"Woof! Woof! Woof!" Juniper was excited also.

Chapter 12 - Friends Forever

We went back to The Smoky Mountains Wild Animal Rescue every week for the rest of the summer. Dad gave me permission to cross the creek now that he was friends with Alice and Dan Baxter.

We would sit on the floor and Alice would tell us stories about all the wild animals they rescued in Miami. We sat there and listened to her for hours.

Sometimes Dad would take us and stay so that Alice would allow us to actually play with Cinnamon and Kiki.

Cinnamon loved to be petted. She would purr just like a kitty cat. She was so sweet and gentle. Alice told us how they tried to teach Cinnamon to hunt. She would not even kill a mouse!

That is why they could not return her to the wild. She would not have survived on her own.

"We are the luckiest kids in the world!" Gaby said jumping up and down, "I can't believe we get to play with a real Florida Panther!"

"Yes, we are lucky," I agreed. "This is so, so special."

Never in my wildest dreams could I have imagined that I would be able to pet a real Florida Panther.

We became very good friends that summer. Juniper and Kiki loved each other. The minute Kiki saw Juni she would run to her and hug her. After a while they would start running around and chasing each other.

One day we were outside our house getting ready to go to see Cinnamon and Kiki and suddenly Juniper started barking and scratching the front door.

"Juni, what do you want?" I asked her. "Did you forget something?"

I opened the door, and she ran inside. She was back in two seconds. She was holding her red monkey in her mouth.

"Juniper you are so sweet!" I hugged her. "You remember Kiki likes your red monkey!"

When Kiki saw the red monkey, she went crazy. She would not stop kissing Juniper. From that day on Juni always took the red monkey to play with Kiki.

"Juni you are going to miss Kiki when we go back to Miami." I told her. "You have become such good friends."

"Woof! Woof! Woof!" Juniper barked in agreement.

"I am going to miss all of you when you go back home." Alice told us, "I don't know what I am going to do with Cinnamon and Kiki. They are going to be so sad."
"We'll be back in winter." I told Alice. "We will miss you too."
We all got very serious.

"Sophie, when do you go back to Miami?" Aiden asked me. "We have to go back to New York in a couple of days."
"I have to go back to Miami in two weeks. My mom likes to spend some of the summer vacation with me. We love going to the beach together and she always wants me home for my birthday." I continued, "are you coming back for Christmas?"
"Yes, we will be back with our parents." Ben said, "we convinced them to spend Christmas here instead of going skiing."
"Good, I'll be back for Christmas vacation and Gaby comes back every Christmas also. It will be fun."

We were quiet walking back home. I am sure we were all thinking what an amazing summer this had been. Even Juniper and Rocco were quiet.

Suddenly Ben said, "let's go to the cave!"

"Yes, let's go," I said, running ahead.

"Let's see who gets there first," Gaby challenged us. She was always the fastest one. She was so fast she could be an Olympic runner. Gaby was out of sight in a flash.

"I win!" Gaby shouted when she got to the cave.

She always amazed me. She was as fast as lightning!

We were all out of breath from running uphill. We sat inside the cave to catch our breath.

"I love it here," I said.

"Yes, it is just perfect!" Gaby agreed.

Juniper looked at us and barked.

I knew exactly what she was thinking.

"Yes Juni, you are right this is where it all began!"

The End

ABOUT THE AUTHOR

 *Irene Hernández is a teacher and writer. She loves children, animals, the ocean, mountains, traveling and reading.*

Her love for children, animals, and reading inspired her to write the **JUST JUNIPER Adventures.**

Irene lives in Miami, Florida where she enjoys going to the beach as often as possible.

THE ILLUSTRATOR

Silvia María de la Fé is a very talented artist. She was encouraged by her sisters Lulú and Irene (the author) to follow her passion.

Now retired, she is enjoying drawing, painting and illustrating the ***JUST JUNIPER Series!*** *Silvia lives in Palm Bay, with her son Joey.*

Scan the QR code below:

Please leave a review.

JUST JUNIPER- The First Adventure (Book 1)

The Mystery of the Mountain Lion Tracks(Book 2)

The Secret at the Lighthouse (Book 3)

Dolphins to the Rescue (Book 4)

Twin Trouble at Turtle Top (Book 5)

The Disappearing Snowman (Book 6)

Dog Day at The Deering Estate (Book 7)

The Royal Corgis (Book 8)

Barney's Big Surprise (Book 9)

Juniper in New York City (Book 10)

Lost in Wynwood (Book 11)

Mystery on the Natchez Trace (Book 12)

JUNIPER !

She's smart...

She's brave...

She' sweet...

She always saves the day!

JUST JUNIPER ADVENTURES

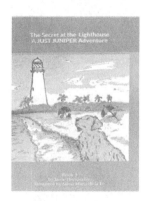

Read all the JUST JUNIPER Books!

Go on more adventures with

JUNIPER!

JUST JUNIPER ADVENTURES

Have fun with JUNIPER!

JUST JUNIPER Activity Books

JUST JUNIPER ADVENTURES
Activity Book 1

Puzzles! Mazes! Word Searches!

Crossword Puzzles! Coloring!

Just Juniper Adventures
Activity Book 2

Just Juniper Adventures
Activity Book 3

Have fun with JUNIPER!

Sketchbooks/Journals

Sketchbooks/Journals

Sketchbooks/Journals

Scan the QR code below:

Please leave a review.

Made in the USA
Las Vegas, NV
08 December 2023

82310252R00059